For the man who really does have Yes
Days with his grandkids—my dad
—A.K.R.

Thanks to Cramer-Krasselt, for the
inspiration, and to my wife, Jan, for
twenty-five years of yeses
—T.L.

kook productions
amy krouse rosenthal & tom lichtenheld

ISBN 978-0-545-33080-0

Text copyright © 2009 by Amy Krouse Rosenthal.
Illustrations copyright © 2009 by Tom Lichtenheld.
All rights reserved. Published by Scholastic Inc.,
557 Broadway, New York, NY 10012, by arrangement with
HarperCollins Children's Books, a division of HarperCollins
Publishers. SCHOLASTIC and associated logos are trademarks
and/or registered trademarks of Scholastic Inc.

12 11 10 9 8 7 6 5 4 3 2 1   11 12 13 14 15 16/0

Printed in the U.S.A.   08

This edition first printing, January 2011

Typography by Jeanne L. Hogle

Today is my FAVORITE day of the year!

Yes Day!

Amy Krouse Rosenthal & Tom Lichtenheld

SCHOLASTIC INC.
New York Toronto London Auckland
Sydney Mexico City New Delhi Hong Kong

Just watch, you'll see what I mean. . . .

Can I please have
pizza for breakfast?

Can I use
your hair gel?

Say "cheese."

Can I clean my room
tomorrow?

Can I pick?

Can we get ice cream?

Can I eat lunch outside?

Can we have a food fight?

Can we invent our own game?

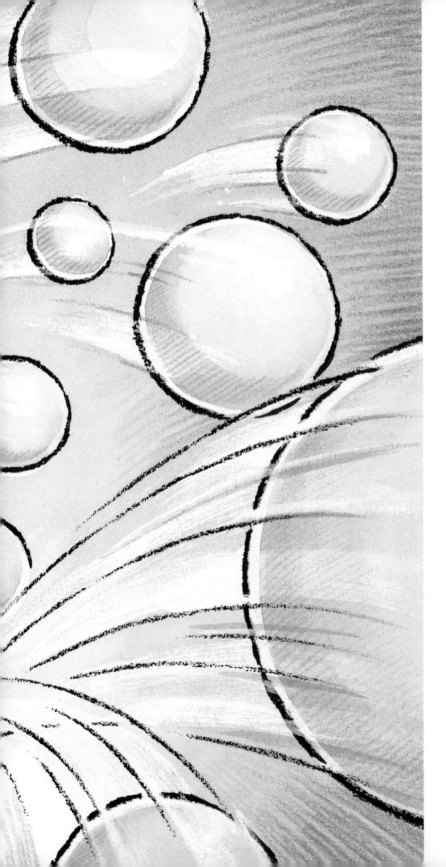

Can I have a
piggyback ride?

Can Mario come over for dinner?

Can we stay up *really* late?

Does this day have to end?

The End
(of Yes Day)

See you again next year!